nickelodeon

TEENAGE MUTANT NINJA TURTLES

MUTANT MAYHEM!

Adapted by Matthew J. Gilbert

Based on the teleplays
"The Gauntlet" and "Panic in the Sewers"
by Joshua Sternin and Jeffrey Ventimilia

RANDOM HOUSE 🏠 NEW YORK

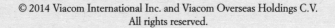

Published in the United States by Random House Children's Books,
a division of Random House LLC, 1745 Broadway, New York, NY 10019,
and in Canada by Random House of Canada Limited, Toronto, LLC,
Penguin Random House Companies. Random House and the colophon
are registered trademarks of Random House LLC. Nickelodeon, Teenage
Mutant Ninja Turtles, and all related titles, logos, and characters are
trademarks of Viacom International Inc. and Viacom Overseas Holdings
C.V. Based on characters created by Peter Laird and Kevin Eastman.

randomhouse.com/kids

ISBN 978-0-385-37433-0

Printed in the United States of America
10 9 8 7 6 5 4 3 2 1

CHAPTER 1

April O'Neil couldn't quite explain it, but for the past few days, she'd felt like she was being followed.

Her walk home was never this quiet. On a normal day, she would have seen her neighborhood shopkeepers out sweeping their sidewalks. She would have yelled hello to Mr. Murakami at the noodle shop. She would have seen some kids from school killing time before curfew. But this was no normal day.

A dark shadow suddenly passed over her.

Something IS following me! she realized in a panic.

Soaring high above her was a huge birdlike

creature with deformed wings. It swooped down at her, its razor-sharp talons ready to tear through any obstacle in its way.

April started running. Trying to throw the creature off her trail, she changed course and ducked into a side street.

If I can just find a place to hide, she told herself, *I'll be safe. . . .*

But she could feel the creature getting closer, its wild shrieks echoing off the buildings.

As April rounded a corner, a streak of sun lit up the building ahead. It was a bank, and its doors were wide open! April sprinted inside past the crowd of customers and took cover behind the building's bulletproof windows. She braced for the worst. . . .

But nothing happened. April slowly peeked outside. There was no sign of the monster. Just an empty street. Had she imagined the whole thing?

She sighed with relief, but then—

Wham! Something smacked into the window. It slid down the glass, stunned. The bank customers rushed over to see what the commotion was.

April just stood there, completely shocked—

the creature, her winged stalker, was *very* real. It appeared to be a giant pigeon with grimy feathers and a hooked beak. But this wasn't an ordinary bird. It was a scientifically engineered combination of pigeon *and* man, a mutant unlike any she'd seen before. And for a girl whose best friends were four mutant turtles, that was definitely saying something!

Looking back into April's eyes, the strange mutant hesitated and then flew away.

As he disappeared into the sky, April watched in disbelief. "My life has gotten really weird."

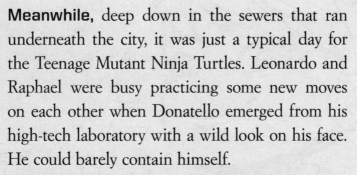

Meanwhile, deep down in the sewers that ran underneath the city, it was just a typical day for the Teenage Mutant Ninja Turtles. Leonardo and Raphael were busy practicing some new moves on each other when Donatello emerged from his high-tech laboratory with a wild look on his face. He could barely contain himself.

"Check it out, guys!" Donnie exclaimed. "We are about to take our *ninjutsu* to a whole new level!"

That took Raph's attention away from sparring. Leo used the opportunity to knock him back on his shell with a swift leg-sweep.

"Cool, Donnie," Leo casually replied, dusting off his hands and crossing his arms.

Donnie opened his palm to reveal a mysterious egg-shaped object. "Last night, I figured out how to make . . . ninja smoke bombs!" he said cheerfully, throwing one to the floor.

As soon as it landed, Donnie disappeared in a puff of purple-black smoke and reappeared on the other side of the *dojo*!

"Whoa . . . ," Leo and Raph said in amazement.

Knowing he had his brothers' complete attention, Donnie revealed his secret ninja-smoke-bomb recipe. "To make them, I carefully drill two holes in an eggshell without cracking it," he explained as he displayed another bomb. "Then I slowly blow out the contents, wait for the inside to dry, pour in flash powder, and seal both holes with wax."

But all Raph heard was "Blah, blah, science, blah." He stared at Donnie's tiny homemade explosive like it was a shiny new toy. "Do it again!" he demanded.

Donnie carefully guarded his creation from Raph. "What I'm trying to tell you," he clarified, "is they take a long time to make, so only use them sparingly."

Suddenly, Michelangelo piped up from the kitchen. "I'm making breakfast!" he announced. "Who wants omelets?"

"Omelets?" A look of concern came over Donnie's face.

"Mikey, don't!" he cried—a second before an explosion shook the kitchen. Once the smoke cleared, Mikey stumbled out to the others in a state of confusion.

"I think that was a rotten egg," Mikey said. He eyed all the eggs in the bowl he was carrying. They looked normal enough to him.

"Those aren't eggs, Mikey," Donnie corrected him. "They're ninja smoke bombs."

Mikey grinned from ear to ear. "No way!" he said, mesmerized.

Raph, Leo, and Donnie watched in nervous anticipation as Mikey grabbed another smoke bomb from the top of the pile. He threw three of them down in rapid succession, using them to camouflage his movements as he zipped around the lair.

Disappearing and reappearing around the room, Mikey declared, *"THIS . . . is the best day . . . of my life!"*

"Stop!" Donnie pleaded.

And in a puff of purple smoke, Mikey materialized right beside him. "I love you, man. Seriously," he gushed, giving Donnie a huge bro-hug.

Before Donnie could reply, the sound of footsteps startled them to attention. Someone was barging into the lair. . . .

It was April. And she looked terrified.

"Guys! Guys!" she started, trying to catch her breath. "You'll never believe what happened to me!"

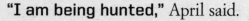

CHAPTER 3

"**I am being hunted,**" April said.

The Turtles hung on her every word.

"By"—she paused for dramatic effect—"*a giant pigeon.*"

Raph couldn't help it. He burst out laughing. It was only after getting death stares from everyone that he asked, "What? I can't be the only one who finds that funny."

"It's *not* funny, Raph!" Donnie scolded. "There's a creature out there trying to hurt *my* April. . . ."

Realizing what he'd just said in front of his secret crush, Donnie quickly tried to save face. "*Our* April!"

That was awkward! Donnie could feel the blush rising in his cheeks.

Thankfully, Mikey chimed in. "This is serious. I'd better get Splinter," he decided, readying a fresh smoke bomb in his hand.

Leo tried to stop him. "We don't really need—"

POOF! Mikey vanished in a cloud of ninja smoke to retrieve their wise sensei.

The other Turtles rolled their eyes. Another smoke bomb wasted.

Later, the Turtles and Splinter listened as April described the hideous pigeon-man. "His talons were razor sharp! He would have torn me to pieces if he hadn't slammed into the glass!"

Raph started laughing again. "A giant pigeon," he mumbled. "That's hilarious, right?" He looked up from the monster-movie magazine he was reading to see that, still, no one else found it funny.

"Really?" he asked. "Just me."

"Raphael!" Splinter snapped, swatting Raph with his cane. "Clearly April is upset."

"Yeah, dude. That's so insensitive," Mikey agreed. "Do you need a tissue?" he asked April gently.

"I think I'm okay," she answered.

"I'll get you a tissue." Mikey vanished via smoke bomb. After a moment he emerged from the purple fog right beside April. "We don't have any tissues. Can I make you some soup?"

Frustrated, Donnie grabbed Mikey's arm before he could throw down another smoke bomb. "Stop it!" Donnie yelled. He then turned his attention back to April. "Don't worry," he assured her. "We won't let anything happen to you."

"Donnie's right," Leo said. And like any good leader, he already had a plan. "We're going to set a trap for this pigeon-man and make sure he never bothers you again."

"Well, I know what we can use as bait," Donnie added.

"Bread crumbs!" Mikey suggested.

Donnie didn't even dignify that with a response.

"Pigeons eat bread crumbs," Mikey muttered. "I *meant* April."

"You're going to let him eat April?!" Mikey shrieked, rushing to her defense. "I thought you liked her!"

"Yeah!" April exclaimed indignantly. She wanted no part of this so-called plan. "I'm trying to avoid this mutant bird-man, not volunteer to be his prey!"

"Don't sweat it," Donnie said coolly. "We've got your back."

Leo could understand April's concern, but he was sure they could protect her. How much trouble could one bird-man cause?

In his most heroic voice, Leo commanded, "All right, Mighty Mutants, let's do this!"

"*Mighty Mutants?*" Raph repeated in a mocking tone. "What, Dancing Dorks was already taken?"

Leo ignored him. "Let's just go."

"Wait! We do not yet know what you are facing," Splinter warned, entering the room. "You should study your enemy before confronting him."

"With all due respect, Sensei, it's a pigeon," Leo said.

As a wise ninja master, Splinter knew that even the greatest of warriors could sometimes confuse arrogance with confidence. "What you know is dangerous to your enemy," Splinter told him. "What you *think* you know is dangerous to you. I fear you are all becoming overconfident."

"Sensei, in the past few months, we've taken down giant spiders, plant creatures, alien robots, and an army of ninjas," Leo said, reassuring his master. "Maybe we're not overconfident. Maybe we're just *that* good."

Leo led them all out of the *dojo* and up to the streets. It was time for the Teenage Mutant Ninja Turtles to *shell shock* this mystery mutant and keep their winning streak alive!

CHAPTER 4

Meanwhile, at the Shredder's secret lair, Chris Bradford—martial arts celebrity and top ninja assassin—found himself staring into the jaws of an angry *Akita Inu* guard dog. The beast, named Hachiko, was vicious, bloodthirsty, and very hungry. And it was snarling at Bradford as though he was its dinner.

Trying to calm the dog, Bradford slowly reached out his hand. "It's okay, Hachiko. I'm not gonna hurt you."

But Hachiko could feel his fear. And that made Bradford an easy target. The beast clamped its jaws down on Bradford's hand. Hard.

Sharp pain shot through Bradford's arm, and he yanked his hand back, but the damage was already done: Hachiko had punctured the skin and drawn blood.

At that moment, a frightening yet familiar voice came booming from the shadows. "Hachiko is not pleased with you. . . ."

Bradford lowered his head in shame as the man behind that voice came closer.

"Nor am I," the voice continued. It was Shredder! The armored ninja warlord stepped forward into the shafts of moonlight that illuminated the lair. He looked down on Bradford with great disappointment.

Fortunately for Bradford, he wasn't the only one in the hot seat. Xever, Shredder's other top assassin, was also on his knees being scolded.

"I entrusted you both with the task of destroying Splinter and his loathsome Turtles," Shredder went on, marching toward his throne. He took a moment to savor his anger, then turned his attention to Bradford. "I spent years molding you in my image, teaching you my darkest secrets. And you shame me with your incompetence."

The look of humiliation on Bradford's face told Shredder that his words had hurt the man deeply. But Xever found it amusing. Seeing the so-called Golden Boy of the Foot Clan get disciplined made him chuckle with glee.

"And *you*!" Shredder yelled, getting in Xever's face. "I should have left you to rot in that prison where I found you."

This startled Xever into silence.

Before Shredder could say another word, Bradford spoke. "The Turtles have been lucky so far, but it won't last forever."

Trying to save face, Xever added, "The next time we meet, I promise you—"

"Enough!" interrupted Shredder. "I am weary of your excuses."

The ruthless lord of the Foot Clan finally took his seat on the throne, his purple cape spilling around him. Behind his metallic face mask, he glowered at Bradford and Xever. He had already given them two chances to eliminate the Turtles— and they'd failed miserably.

The time had come for him to take matters into his own hands.

"I will now destroy the Turtles myself," snarled Shredder.

CHAPTER 5

Later that night, April wandered the city's abandoned streets and alleys in an attempt to lure the pigeon-man. She knew the Turtles were waiting in the shadows, ready to protect her, but she was still mad about this whole *bait* thing. And she let everyone know it.

"Here I am walking around in the big city," she announced loudly, "all alone. I sure hope no crazy pigeon-man sneaks up on me. That would be the *last* thing I'd want."

Donnie, impatient, popped up from his hiding place. "What are you doing?" he barked.

"You wanted me to be bait," she said. "I'm bait."

"That's not how bait talks."

"How do you know how bait talks?" she asked.

"I know bait *doesn't* talk *back*," he answered.

"Ohhhhhh!" the other Turtles teased, momentarily popping their heads up from the darkness.

"Oh, no you didn't!" Mikey added.

Donnie pleaded with April. "Just act natural," he insisted. He gave her a supportive smile before returning to the shadows with the other Turtles.

April was alone again.

"Here I am, acting natural," she sighed. "Totally defenseless against any hideous mutant pigeons that might happen upon me."

April was beginning to think this was a giant waste of time—until she heard a loud shriek coming from the sky. She looked up and screamed.

"Now!" Leo shouted.

Donnie activated a strange device that looked like a kitchen mixer. It was an extremely powerful electroshock weapon.

The jolt froze the pigeon-man in midair, his talons just inches away from April's face! With the help of a few thousand volts, the Turtles were able to wrestle the stunned mutant to the ground.

April turned her attention to Donnie. "And you said I wasn't good bait," she bragged.

Certain their captive was no longer a threat, Leo signaled for his brothers to let the bird-man up. And that was when they all got a good look at it under the streetlights: the blue jeans, the way it stood on two legs, the vulnerability behind its eyes—it was the most human mutant they'd ever seen.

"Start talking, pigeon-man," Leo demanded.

"I have a name," the bird-man squawked.

"Yeah, we just don't care what it is," Raph taunted.

"It's Pete," the bird-man grumbled.

"Why were you trying to hurt April, Pete?" Leo asked.

"I don't want to hurt her," Pigeon Pete explained. "I was just bringing her a message . . . from her father."

"My father?" April said, her voice trembling. She hadn't seen him in weeks, and his whereabouts had been a mystery ever since the Kraang, a race of evil, extradimensional aliens, abducted him without explanation.

"How do you know my father?" she asked.

"We were both 'guests' of the Kraang," Pigeon Pete replied, looking serious. "They poured some ooze on me and turned me into this."

April gasped. "That must have been horrible, being turned into a . . . pigeon."

"Actually," Pigeon Pete corrected her, "I started out as a pigeon."

"Told you the bread crumbs would have worked," Mikey said.

"You've got bread crumbs?!" Pigeon Pete clucked excitedly. Unable to control his inner-animal urges, he grabbed Mikey and started searching his shell for any sign of food.

"Um . . . my father?" April reminded him.

"Right!" Pigeon Pete let go of Mikey and pulled a videophone from his pants pocket. April took it from him as a recorded message from her father began to play on its screen.

"Something terrible is about to happen," her father warned. "I don't know what, but it's extremely important that you get out of the city as soon as you can."

Then, as if that might be the last time he'd ever speak to her, her father looked into the camera and said, "I love you, April."

And with that, his video message ended.

"I love you, too, Daddy," April said with tears in her eyes.

Leo shared a look of concern with his brothers. It was clear the Kraang were plotting something catastrophic, but what?

"Pete, do you have any idea what he's talking about?" Leo asked.

"I'm just the messenger," Pigeon Pete replied.

"Well, whatever it is," Donnie said, turning to April, "we've got to get you out of the city."

"I'm not going anywhere without my dad," April announced.

Donnie tried to reason with her. "But you heard him. Something terrible is going to happen."

"Then we'd better hurry," she stubbornly replied.

The Turtles had been around April long enough to know when she wasn't going to budge on something. It was time for a rescue mission—whether the Turtles liked it or not!

"Pete, can you tell us where the Kraang are holding him?" Leo asked.

"I can," Pigeon Pete answered. "But it's gonna cost you a lot of bread."

For a split second, Leo worried about how much cash they'd need to buy Pigeon Pete off, until he remembered. "We're talking about actual bread, right?"

"Yeah. Sourdough," Pigeon Pete told him.

"Done," Leo said.

"Let's roll!" Mikey yelled, throwing down a celebratory smoke bomb.

Together they moved in formation toward the Kraang's hideout—completely unaware that a group of shadowy figures were watching them from the rooftops.

CHAPTER 7

While the Turtles were searching for the Kraang's secret hideout, Bradford and Xever were looking at the face of a hideous fish.

Xever skillfully scooped it out of its algae-covered fish tank. What he held in his hands was an Asian snakehead fish, with slimy red-purple scales and a large, fang-lined mouth. This tiny Chinatown fish market called it a delicacy—but Bradford thought it looked more like a monster.

"That's the ugliest thing I've ever seen," Bradford said as he stared at the snakehead gasping for air. Then he looked at Xever and added, "Present company excluded."

Just before the fish could flop out of his hands, Xever tossed it to the vendor, signaling him to wrap it up for dinner.

Bradford took a deep breath. "So, we have a problem," he said.

"No, *you* have a problem," Xever replied.

"We've both failed Master Shredder. Can you live with that shame?" Bradford asked.

His question was met with an angry silence as the reality of the situation finally dawned on Xever. He prided himself on his reputation with the ninja underworld. To be remembered as a failure would undo all the villainous victories he'd worked so hard for.

"If I had the opportunity, I would crush those Turtles like bugs!" Xever hissed.

Just then, Bradford's cell phone chimed on with an alert.

"What's that?" Xever asked.

Bradford grinned from ear to ear as he read the message on the screen. It was a text from one of their Foot Soldier spies. He had a lock on the Turtles' exact location.

"Opportunity." Bradford smiled.

It was time for revenge—and redemption!

CHAPTER 8

From the outside, the Kraang's facility looked like any other industrial building after midnight. There were no lights on and no signs of life— absolutely nothing to attract the attention of any suspicious earthling who might wander by.

The Turtles found a small door in the roof of the building. As Donnie tinkered with the lock, everyone else focused on April. No one said it, but they were all thinking the same thing: There was no way of knowing what condition her father would be in after weeks of being held prisoner by an alien race. He could be badly injured, brain-washed, or *worse.* The Turtles knew they would have to bring their ninja A-game if they were going to rescue him.

The hatch lock opened with a *clank*. "Piece of cake," Donnie said confidently.

"Let's do this!" April said, pushing her way to the front.

"We need you to wait here, April," Leo reminded her, blocking her way.

"Are you crazy?" she protested. "My dad's in there!"

"Along with who knows how many Kraang! Leave it to the pros."

April felt defeated. Being excluded from her father's rescue was not an option. She gave Leo a hard stare and tried to plead her case.

"I can't just do nothing," she said.

"You won't be doing nothing," he informed her, handing her a rope in the darkness. "We need you to lower this rope when we give you the signal."

It was clear Leo wouldn't change his mind. With a sigh, April took the rope and watched the Turtles disappear down the hatch.

The inside of the Kraang's facility resembled a space station. The titanium walls hummed with bright-pink energy as Kraang computers processed information at lightning speed. There were muta-gen labs, mutant testing areas, prison cells, power cores, and command centers—all under one roof.

The Kraang-droids—the shiny exoskeletons that housed the slimy Kraang brainlike things—patrolled the corridors with military precision, blasters charged up and ready to fire.

The Turtles began to stealthily drop in, one by one: first Leo, then Donnie; then Raph; and then Mikey landed with a loud *thud!*

A droid spun around, putting Mikey in its sights. With no time to react, Mikey could only cover his face and wince, afraid of what would come next. The barrel of the droid's blaster illu-minated, readying a bolt. But at the last moment, Raph sprang into action, burying his *sai* into its robotic head. The Kraang-droid seized up, and then its body exploded in a mess of metal and sparks.

That was close, Mikey thought. Opening his eyes, he smiled at Raph.

But instead of smiling back, Raph bopped him hard on the head—a painful reminder to be more careful next time!

The Turtles moved through the lab in formation, watching each other's shells. They knew they had to keep their eyes peeled for any sign of April's dad. And they needed to get deeper inside the facility.

Up ahead, two droids were waiting by an air-locked door. Leo paused and motioned for his brothers to wait for the robots to gain access. One droid rapidly keyed in a code. Once the entrance opened, Leo rolled forward, sneaked up behind the droids, and bashed their heads together, knocking them out in one swift move!

A third Kraang-droid pulled his blaster and aimed at Leo. Raph dropped that bot by throwing a *sai* right between its eyes.

They were in!

But *what* they were in was anyone's guess. It seemed like some sort of control room.

It made Mikey feel as though he were in a sci-fi movie—especially with the real-life alien just a few feet away.

They all took a closer look at the Kraang housed in the bot. It was a gelatinous, brainlike creature that appeared dazed and confused. But after a moment, its tentacles began to move, and the Kraang roared back to life!

Without hesitation, Leo stepped up and punched the alien's lights out for good. It was one KO'd Kraang!

The Turtles exchanged looks. They were pleased they'd made it this far, but now it was time to find April's dad—and to find out what the Kraang were up to.

Leo gave the others their orders. "Donnie, hack into the system and see what you can find out about the Kraang's plot."

Donnie nodded, his hands itching to touch the keys in front of him.

"Raph," Leo continued, "you're with me."

He then locked eyes with Mikey—who waited with a big, goofy smile.

"Mikey . . . stay with Donnie," he said.

"Why do I always get stuck with Mikey?" Donnie asked.

"I don't want him, and I'm in charge," Leo said matter-of-factly.

"Hey!" Mikey shouted in frustration.

Completely ignoring Mikey, Donnie suggested, "Well, then make Raph take Mikey!"

"Over my dead body!" Raph piped up.

"Hey! You know, I'm starting to think nobody wants to be with me," Mikey said, his feelings hurt. "I'll just go off on my own."

Mikey threw a smoke bomb and—*poof!*—seemed to disappear into thin air. But he didn't manage to go far! A split second later, he came through a door on the other side of the control room.

"That was a closet," he explained.

Leo and Raph were already out the door. "Have fun, you two!" Raph said, shutting the air lock.

Mikey looked around the alien control room like a kid in an arcade.

"What's that button do?" Mikey asked, pointing excitedly.

Donnie smacked his hand away, gritting his teeth. "Don't. Touch. Anything."

Hacking an alien computer mainframe was hard enough, but babysitting Mikey at the same time? This was going to be a challenge.

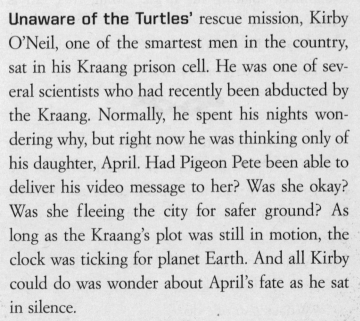

Unaware of the Turtles' rescue mission, Kirby O'Neil, one of the smartest men in the country, sat in his Kraang prison cell. He was one of several scientists who had recently been abducted by the Kraang. Normally, he spent his nights wondering why, but right now he was thinking only of his daughter, April. Had Pigeon Pete been able to deliver his video message to her? Was she okay? Was she fleeing the city for safer ground? As long as the Kraang's plot was still in motion, the clock was ticking for planet Earth. And all Kirby could do was wonder about April's fate as he sat in silence.

Then he heard a voice on the other side of the wall. "Mr. O'Neil? Are you in here?"

He looked through the small window of his cell door and was shocked to see the Teenage Mutant Ninja Turtles!

"You're the turtles who rescued my daughter!" he cried. "Is she okay?"

"She's fine," Leo answered, trying to break the door lock. "She's right outside."

"You mean she's still in the city?!" Kirby exclaimed, shaking his head. "Man, that girl is stubborn."

"Yeah," Leo admitted. "We've noticed."

Leo went to work on the lock.

Back in the Kraang's control room, things weren't going any better for Donnie. He had to use every ounce of his ninja speed to smack Mikey's hand away from the array of buttons on the computer console.

"What's that one do?" Mikey asked.

Smack! "I don't know," Donnie replied.

"What's *that one* do?"

Smack! Smack! "I don't know!"

"What's *THAT ONE* do??"

Smack! Smack! Smack!

"I DON'T KNOW!"

Not being able to touch anything was making Mikey want to touch everything. He noticed a stream of digital lights flowing up toward another button.

"Ooooh, that one's pretty!" he exclaimed.

Donnie snapped. "Just stop it!" he yelled, slamming his fists down in frustration, which made the room go dark.

After a moment, one computer screen lit up.

"I'm in!" Donnie said excitedly.

The Kraang's files were now an open book—and it wouldn't have been possible without Mikey.

"You're welcome," Mikey teased.

But the celebration would have to wait. As Donnie tried to make sense of the Kraang's secret plans unfolding on the monitor, a grave look came over his face. He might not have fully understood complex alien technology, but he knew a bomb when he saw one.

And he was staring at the blueprints for the biggest one he'd ever seen.

All he could say was "Uh-oh."

Despite Leo's best lock-picking efforts, Kirby O'Neil was still trapped in his cell. There was no sign of any Kraang-droids, but Raph knew they were running out of time. "Since it's taking Leo forever to pick that lock—"

"I'm working on it!" Leo said impatiently.

"—maybe you can tell us what the heck's the deal with the Kraang?" Raph continued, ignoring Leo.

Kirby took a moment. The Turtles were protecting his daughter and trying to rescue him. They deserved some answers. But were they ready for the truth?

"They're aliens from another *dimension,*" he began. "When they came here, they brought the mutagen with them."

That gave Leo pause. The Kraang were the ones who had brought the mutagen? The same stuff that had mutated Master Splinter all those years ago? The same ooze that had mutated *them*? Leo understood the idea of an alien race wanting to destroy humanity, but choosing to mutate it into something else? Why?

"What's the point of turning people into monsters?" Leo asked Kirby.

"The mutagen doesn't work the way they thought it would," Kirby explained. "Apparently, the physical laws of their universe are different from ours."

And with that, the reasons behind the Kraang's kidnapping of Kirby suddenly became clear to Leo. "They're grabbing scientists to help them modify the ooze," he concluded.

"Wow! You figured it out!" Raph mocked. "How's that lock coming?"

Now it was Leo who was ignoring Raph. "So what do they want the ooze to do?" he asked Kirby.

Kirby sighed. "I wish I knew."

Suddenly, Raph and Leo heard footsteps coming from around the corner. They braced for the worst!

It was only Mikey and Donnie.

"Leo! Raph! They've planted a mutagen bomb downtown!" Donnie said, panicked. "They're going to use it to disperse ooze over the entire city!" Then, seeing April's dad for the first time, he tried to compose himself and added, "Oh, hi, Mr. O'Neil! Your daughter's *really* nice."

Leo had to stay focused and think. Breaking Kirby out seemed impossible. Soon more Kraang would come looking for them. And to top it all off, they now had to deal with an intergalactic bomb threat. This mission was spiraling out of control fast, but Leo kept calm. He knew if the Turtles wanted to save the day, they were going to have to face these challenges one at a time—starting with *this lock.*

"We have to disarm that bomb," Leo said, still tinkering with the cell door. "If I could just get this stupid door open!"

That gave Mikey a bright idea. "Have you tried *this?*" he asked, pushing a random button on the wall.

"Noooo!" everyone else yelled.

But it was too late. Mikey had just triggered an alarm.

"And that's why no one wants to be with you!" Raph remarked.

They could hear the clanging feet of Kraang-droids as they marched down the hall.

There was no time for Leo to panic. He felt a small lever move inside the lock, and then— *click*—the cell door popped open!

"Got it! Let's move!" Leo ordered, grabbing Kirby from his cell.

With April's dad in tow, the Turtles ran down the corridor as fast as they could, dodging blaster fire from the approaching Kraang-droids.

Quickly, Leo led them back to the original rooftop hatch. As planned, he started doing dove calls, hoping this would cue April to lower the rope. But it was no use. With the alarm blaring over the PA and energy bolts whizzing in every direction, she couldn't hear his signal.

More blaster fire cut through the air. The Turtles were surrounded by Kraang-droids!

CHAPTER 10

"April!" Raph shouted over the deafening sound of blaster fire. "Throw the rope!"

From the rooftop, April dropped the rope down as promised and got her first real look at the chaos inside the facility. She saw the Turtles taking cover behind a barrier of wooden crates. She saw the Kraang-droids closing in. She saw Raph cut through a bot with one of his *sais,* causing its blaster to fall to the ground.

And for the first time since he'd been kidnapped, April saw her father, Kirby O'Neil.

"Dad!" she cried out.

"April!" he called back.

Kirby couldn't believe he was looking at his daughter's face again. The only thing that had gotten him through this kidnapping ordeal was the hope that he would be reunited with her. But the reunion he'd been dreaming about wasn't happening the way he wanted. He didn't want her to risk her life for him! He had hoped she would flee the city. He'd hoped she would escape the Kraang. Now he hoped she would forgive him for what he was about to do.

He looked at the blaster that had fallen near Raph's feet.

Kirby picked it up and put his finger on the trigger.

"Mr. O'Neil, what are you doing?" Leo asked him.

"Save my daughter. Save the city," he told Leo with a strange determination.

April couldn't hear what he was saying to Leo, but something seemed wrong.

And that was when she saw her father charge into battle.

"Daddy, no!" she screamed.

And to everyone's surprise, Kirby began firing a barrage of energy bolts at the Kraang-droids to hold them off. It was enough of a diversion to help the Turtles—and his daughter—escape.

Leo never liked to leave a man behind, but he knew there was no other option. "Go! Go!" he commanded, ordering the Turtles to climb to safety.

"We can't leave him here!" Donnie insisted.

"We don't have a choice!" Leo yelled.

The other Turtles hated to admit it, but they knew Leo was right. They were outnumbered and outgunned. One by one, they hurried up the rope to the rooftop.

The Turtles had just made it to April when they saw the Kraang-droids overpower Kirby and drag him back to his cell.

They shared a silence, realizing her father's plan had worked—he had sacrificed his freedom to save their shells!

April couldn't take it. She ran into Donnie's arms, sobbing.

"We'll get him back, April," he said, trying to comfort her. "I promise."

But there was no time to worry about that now. They needed to get April to safety. They needed a new plan. They needed to stop that bomb!

CHAPTER 11

The mutagen bomb was hidden on the rooftop of the Hotel Wolf, one of downtown's premier hotels. Normally, business executives and international tourists would stay on the top floor, but tonight's guests of honor were the Kraang. And those slimy little alien brain-things weren't there for the four-star service. They were preparing to cover the entire city in ooze!

The bomb was behind the hotel's glowing neon sign, carefully guarded by a team of sharpshooting Kraang-droids.

"Kraang, in how many time units known as minutes will the device containing the mutagen that will be spread over the place known as New York be detonated?" one of the droids asked.

"Five—"

Just then, a strange, unknown object flew through the sky and—*KABOOM!*—hit a droid between the eyes, blowing it into a thousand pieces.

Seeing this, the other Kraang-droids fanned out in formation, trying to protect the bomb and determine what was happening. They scanned their surroundings, focusing so hard on their next plan of action, they didn't notice that another projectile had gone airborne.

It was an exploding arrow, shot from a hidden location by the Ninja Turtles. Each of the Turtles was now outfitted with bows and arrows, courtesy of Splinter's ancient ninja armory.

Raph slotted another arrow into his bow and aimed at a Kraang-droid. He pulled back and fired, destroying his target with one clean shot. The vulnerable Kraang leaped out of its damaged exoskeleton, hissing into the shadows.

Two Kraang-droids down, four to go!

Now it was Donnie and Mikey's turn to get in on the archery action. With only a split second to aim, Donnie managed to take out the droid at the bomb's control panel.

Mikey opted for a close-encounter attack. He did a barrel roll onto the rooftop, running directly toward the oncoming Kraang-droids. With impressive speed and ninja reflexes, he dodged blaster fire and rapidly shot down two bots on his own!

And that left the last Kraang-droid for Leo. He somersaulted onto the hotel sign and dropped down with his trusty *katana* blades, slicing the final bot right down the middle!

Now there was nothing between the Turtles and the bomb but dismembered droid parts and a few harmless, slithering Kraang brain-things.

"Okay, Donnie, it's up to you," Leo said.

But as Donnie opened the bomb's access panel, his jaw dropped.

"Uh-oh," he muttered.

There were Kraang symbols, encrypted combinations, and a tangled nest of detonation wires inside. The mutagen tanks gave off a haunting green glow, stressing him out beyond belief.

"Umm . . . Donnie!" Leo said with concern. "You told us you could do this!"

"I didn't count on a design this complex," Donnie admitted.

"They're aliens from another dimension," Leo said firmly. "What did you expect? A big round ball with a lit fuse that said *BOMB*?"

"No, but this is—"

Raph interrupted them, noticing the bomb's countdown clock. "Boy, I sure hope this argument goes on for another four minutes and fifteen seconds!"

Trying to ignore them and focus on the task at hand, Donnie looked down at the bomb control panel. Then back at the countdown clock. Then back at the panel. This wasn't going to be easy.

With his brothers watching his every move, Donnie gently reached out to touch the trip wire. . . .

"Careful!" Leo shouted, startling Donnie.

Donnie shot him a look. He wiped the sweat from his brow and took a deep breath. He resumed reaching for the wires when—

"Watch out for those wires!" Raph warned.

"You guys are *not* helping!" Donnie shouted.

Mesmerized by all the buttons *just waiting to be pushed,* Mikey offered his suggestion: "What if we just pushed *this* button?"

Raph grabbed his hand. "Don't you think you've pushed enough buttons tonight?" he growled.

As the numbers continued to tick away, Leo couldn't take it anymore. "Donnie, you're gonna have to speed this up."

Donnie snapped. "I can't work with all this pressure!" he yelled.

Something caught Leo's attention out of the corner of his eye. He turned to see that they weren't the only ones watching Donnie try to defuse this bomb. "Um . . . that might be a problem," Leo muttered.

The Turtles looked up in unison to see two figures on the rooftop.

It was Bradford and Xever—Shredder's top two henchmen! And they were ready for a fight!

The bomb might not have gone off yet, but the Turtles now found them- selves in a seriously *explosive* situation!

CHAPTER 12

The sounds of power punches and karate kicks distracted Donnie as he worked on the bomb. Even though he wasn't in the fight, he felt like his concentration was taking a beating. He glanced up every few seconds to see his brothers facing off against Xever and Bradford in what looked like an epic battle between ninja masters.

With a skillful flip, Xever effortlessly threw Mikey to the side. But just as he was about to finish him off, Leo jumped in and countered with a swift spin kick.

"You guys picked a really bad time for this!" Leo told Xever.

"Oh, sorry for the inconvenience," Xever said sarcastically. "When would you prefer to breathe your last breath?"

As Xever unleashed a roundhouse kick, Leo tried to reason with him. "If that thing goes off, it'll wipe us *all* out!"

Meanwhile, Bradford and Raph were engaged in a battle of blades. Bradford fearlessly swung his *samurai* sword down at Raph's awaiting *sais*. "I'd rather perish with honor than live in shame!" he announced.

Raph saw an opening and knocked the wind out of Bradford with a fierce thrust. He turned and shouted to Donnie, "Will you hurry up and defuse the bomb? We're dealing with a couple of nut-jobs here!"

"Be quiet!" Donnie yelled from the bomb panel, trying to focus.

With a burst of rage, Xever launched a series of lightning-fast attacks on Leo and Mikey. He managed to dodge their weapons and perform a spinning split kick that sent both Turtles flying backward onto their shells.

Leaping away from his own fight with Bradford, Raph somersaulted over to help them out. He rushed Xever, but it was no use. The wiry thug was too fast for Raph's brawling, street-fighting style.

As Bradford swooped down to face Leo and Mikey, Donnie was still racing the countdown clock. Thankfully, all the wires he'd disconnected so far had been ineffective booby traps and decoys.

"Down to two wires," he said to himself. "Which do I cut, black or green?"

"Go for the green!" Mikey yelled from the rumble just as Bradford leveled him with a punch.

Mikey was the last Turtle Donnie wanted to listen to, but he noticed the countdown clock was in the final seconds. The bomb was about to blow! There was no time to disagree with Mikey.

"Eh, why not?" Donnie asked himself, snipping the green wire in half.

Donnie shut his eyes, bracing for impact—

Nothing happened.

He looked up to see the countdown clock frozen in time with one second to go! He had done it—the bomb was defused! The city was safe!

"Guys! Guys!" Donnie called out excitedly. "Mikey was right about something!"

But this was no time to celebrate. On the upper level, where the bomb's mutagen tanks were stowed, Bradford had gained the upper hand against Leo and Mikey. Donnie grabbed his *bo* staff and sprang into action. He surprised Bradford with a jumping strike and bought his bros enough time to get back on their feet. Then he sprinted up behind Xever and Raph and stopped their fistfight with a flurry of ninja moves. With Donnie in the mix, it was clear the Turtles had the edge they needed.

Within moments, Xever and Bradford were up against the tank of mutagen, and they knew they were close to losing this battle.

Leo stepped forward with his *katana* raised. "You are worthy adversaries, but the fight is ours! Lay down your weapons!" he commanded in his best hero voice.

"Never!" yelled Xever.

"You don't have a choice," Leo told them. "You've lost."

Bradford ignored Leo's words, concentrating instead on the strange glowing tanks behind them. Maybe they did have a chance to escape—a chance to turn the tables on the Turtles once and for all. An idea was forming. He tightened his grip on the *samurai* sword and got into position. "If I'm going down, I'm taking you with me!" he threatened.

Bradford turned toward the glass tank that contained the mutagen and plunged his sword into it, shattering the glass. A luminescent geyser of blue-green ooze sprayed out, washing him and Xever away into the darkness.

Under flickering lights, the Turtles watched the mutagen bomb's power source malfunction and shut down for good. All was quiet now on the roof of the Hotel Wolf.

Turning to face his brothers, Leo smiled. "So to sum up: we kicked the butts of the Kraang and Shredder's top henchmen while defusing a bomb and saving the city."

"Yeah, we're not *overconfident,*" Raph said, remembering what Splinter had told them back at the lair.

"We're just that good," Leo bragged.

The Turtles celebrated with an epic high three, beaming over their victory. . . .

Until they heard a deep, menacing voice.

"Your skills are impressive," the voice growled.

The Turtles looked up to see a spiky figure

before them silhouetted against the moon.

"... but they will not save you," the figure went on, jumping down to their level.

The Turtles took in the towering mass of bulging muscles and jagged armor. He moved with unnatural speed and looked at them with a bloodlust that sent a chill up their shells.

CHAPTER 13

The Turtles were frozen by the terrifying vision standing before them.

"Oh man, do you think that's . . . *the* Shredder?" Donnie asked. For weeks, they'd only heard about this monster of a man from Splinter, but now he was a flesh-and-blood threat standing a few feet away. They all noticed the spikes, blades, and gauntlets that covered his armor.

"Well, it's definitely *a* Shredder." Raph smirked.

The Turtles sensed a wicked smile forming beneath the armor on Shredder's face as he crept closer.

"There is undoubtedly a fascinating story in how my old nemesis came to teach *ninjutsu* to four mutant turtles," Shredder snarled. "Perhaps I will let one of you live long enough to tell it."

"You're gonna have to catch us first!" Leo said. "Mikey!"

Mikey had one of his ninja smoke bombs at the ready. "So long, *sucka*!" he yelled, throwing the bomb to the floor—

But nothing happened. No flash charge. No smoke. Just a *splat* and a cracked egg at their feet.

The Turtles all looked at Mikey at once.

"Oops. All right, that one's on me." Mikey smiled sheepishly.

But they weren't smiling back.

And neither was Shredder.

The Turtles had no choice but to face him right there on the rooftop of the Hotel Wolf!

Raph charged first, both *sais* aiming for Shredder's heart. The ironclad ninja master blocked Raph's every move, gracefully catching his *sais* in the spikes of his armor. With a forceful front kick, Shredder booted Raph into the neon hotel sign.

Leo jumped in, bringing his *katanas* down onto Shredder's shoulder spikes. His attacks were faster than Raph's, but it didn't seem to matter—Shredder zipped around him with ease, flicking Leo's *katanas* away and kicking him to the ground with a speedy *kata* combination.

Donnie cried out in horror, "Leo!"

He rushed to his brother's side, finding him dazed and injured. It wasn't every day he saw his older bro—his *leader*—fall to an enemy. Donnie felt his anger swell. Swinging his *bo* staff, he tried to smack Shredder but barely made a dent.

Watching this go down, Mikey decided he was done waiting. He unleashed the secret blade from his *nunchucks* chain and joined Donnie's side for the tag team!

They alternated punches, kicks, and combo attacks—just like they'd practiced back at the *dojo*. Mikey even wrapped his chain around Shredder's arms, but the ninja master slipped out a split second later! He truly lived up to his fearsome legend. It was as if his *ninjutsu* transcended reality.

Donnie and Mikey didn't stand a chance against him. Before they knew it, Shredder flung them both to the ground with brute force.

Not wanting to accept defeat, the Turtles got back on their feet and headed in for more. They were all tired, hurt, and afraid.

And Shredder knew it.

He could *feel* it—the same way animals in the wild could smell someone's fright. He relished this moment, his gauntlet blades projecting from his armor. In a series of slashes, he cut Donnie's weapon in half, overpowered Raph, and pummeled Leo with a crushing blow.

Shredder was just about to finish them off when something suddenly caught his wrist. He looked down to see Mikey's chain!

With all his weight and speed, Mikey used the other end of the chain to rappel down the neon hotel sign that had been towering over them. The moment he began to fall, the chain started to pull—which meant Shredder got yanked up into a trap!

Ensnared, Shredder dangled in the air, unable to break free.

The Turtles took a breath, lucky to be alive. They looked on in wonderment at their master's oldest enemy. He was even more frightening than they'd imagined. Never did they think they'd actually see this fabled warrior up close, let alone face him in battle. Had they achieved the impossible? Had they actually gotten the better of Shredder?

Shredder looked back at them, his eyes narrowing to a fiery gaze. He wasn't used to being thwarted by his opponents. He unsheathed his gauntlet blades once more and sliced through the hotel sign as if it were tissue paper, cutting himself down and pinning Mikey underneath it in the process.

As the other Turtles lifted the severed sign off of Mikey, Shredder landed on the roof with a thud, electric sparks raining down all around him.

Shredder had regained his strength and had the Turtles on the run once again. Soon the only Turtle left standing was Leo. Shredder quickly pinned him against the wall. Holding his blades centimeters away from Leo's eyeballs, Shredder demanded, "Tell me where Splinter is, and I promise your demise will be swift."

In fearless silence, Leo stared down the edge

of Shredder's blade, refusing to reveal anything. He could see the jagged tip getting closer when they both heard a sudden gasp!

Someone—or some*thing*—could be heard choking for air right behind them.

Shredder looked down to see a slimy fish-shaped mutant. It had the face and enlarged mouth of a fish but the arms, hands, and fingers of a man. It was covered in the glowing ooze that had created it.

"Help me," the fish mutant wheezed, its webbed hand reaching out for assistance. Its voice was human and very familiar.

Shredder stared in shock. Just behind him, the Turtles' eyes widened at a second freakish sight. They backed away, spotting another figure being birthed from the mutagen. This one was much larger and was covered in hair. It resembled a gargantuan wolf-man, with one enlarged fist and spike-shaped bones that protruded from its back.

"What is this?" Shredder asked, disgusted.

He couldn't believe his eyes. The mysterious mutagen ooze had worked its magic, transforming two men into monsters.

When Shredder returned his attention to the Turtles, they were gone.

"Noooooo!" Shredder shouted to the skies.

He had lost his targets and accidentally found himself with two new followers. And though their faces were deformed, he somehow knew who they were.

"Xever?" Shredder asked in disbelief. "Brad-ford?!"

These had once been their human names, but Bradford and Xever were no longer people. They had been reborn as . . . mutants!

CHAPTER 14

Later that night, the Turtles returned to their underground lair not as heroes but as survivors. Shredder had left them battered, bruised, and barely able to stand. They sat around, sharing a heavy, uncomfortable silence as April bandaged them up as best she could.

Master Splinter looked at his sons, aware that their pain wasn't just physical, but emotional, too. He could tell that their experience with Shredder had put fear into their hearts. They were doubting themselves and their abilities as ninjas. He wanted to tell them everything would be okay, and that the next time they faced Shredder, things would be different. But he knew that would be a lie. He knew what Shredder was truly capable of—which meant the Turtles were in grave danger.

The Turtles capture a mutant
pigeon with a message for April.

"My life has gotten really weird!"

Shredder is displeased with his
henchmen, Chris Bradford and Xever.

"I am weary of your excuses!
I will destroy the Turtles myself."

Inside the Kraang's fortress, Mikey wonders
what will happen if he pushes a button.

Mikey sets off an alarm—
it's time to battle some bots!

The Kraang are on the march!

Showdown with Shredder!

"Help me," Xever hisses as he transforms into a fishlike mutant.

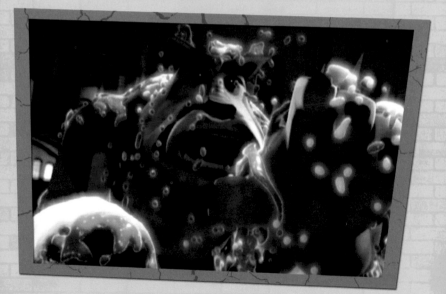

A splash of Kraang mutagen turns Chris Bradford into a canine creature!

Splinter knows the Turtles will need some intense training before they meet Shredder again.

The Turtles earn some rest and relaxation.

Donnie designs an all-terrain patrol
buggy with detachable sidecars.

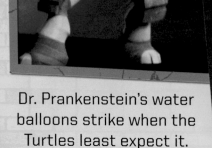

Dr. Prankenstein's water
balloons strike when the
Turtles least expect it.

Raphael is not amused
by Dr. Prankenstein.

Chris Bradford is now Dogpound,
a monstrous mutated villain!

Patrol buggies to the rescue!

"You were all very lucky," Splinter told them.

"I think we define that word differently, Sensei," Raph objected.

"Few have ever faced Shredder and survived," Splinter explained.

"He was just so fast," Mikey said with a wince.

"It was like he was everywhere *at once.*" Donnie shuddered.

Leo gulped. He didn't want to admit defeat, but being in denial meant endangering his own life and the lives of his brothers. With Master Splinter's words echoing in his mind, he knew he had to say something. "You were right about us being overconfident, Sensei," Leo admitted. "There are some things we're just not ready for."

"Perhaps. But that no longer matters," Splinter informed them as he put a comforting hand on Leo's shoulder. "It is clear now that Shredder is a problem that will not go away."

One by one, the Turtles each looked up at their sensei.

"So prepare yourselves, my sons," Splinter advised. "Because as of this moment . . . we are at war."

When the Turtles left the sewers to go out on their nightly patrol, the city was buried in fog. Leo instructed his brothers to keep a tight shell-to-shell formation, watching each other's backs for any sign of danger.

"Shredder could be anywhere," he warned as they entered a darkened alley. "Stay frosty, guys."

"FYI, frost can't accumulate unless it's below freezing," Donnie interjected. "Except during a process called 'radiative cooling.'"

The other Turtles exchanged exasperated looks—this was hardly the time for a science lecture! "Maybe he's got an Off switch somewhere," Mikey jokingly whispered to Raph.

Raph smacked Donnie into silence.

"Found it!" Raph smirked at Mikey.

Raph and Mikey shared a laugh about that, until a cruel voice came out of nowhere, breaking the mood.

"And I found four pathetic Turtles with only seconds to live," the voice echoed.

"Wouldn't want to be them," Mikey remarked with an innocent smile.

"We *are* them!" Raph informed him.

A feeling of dread filled the Turtles. Leo, Donnie, and Raph all drew their weapons.

Realizing that the voice belonged to Shredder, Mikey unholstered his *nunchucks* and began walking backward, completely unaware that he was stepping into a trap.

Shredder's blade-covered arms shot out of the mist and grabbed Mikey, pulling him away into the darkness, Mikey's screams echoing through the night. Before the others could react, Donnie leaped to his brother's defense. He tried his best to bring his *bo* staff down on Shredder's head, but it was no use. It got caught up in the blades and Shredder snapped it in two before kicking Donnie skyward.

"Raph, take him now!" Leo commanded.

The remaining two Turtles charged at Shredder, terrified but determined. With a series of rapid-fire power punches, Shredder deflected their weak attack and catapulted Raph into the surrounding fog.

"No!" Leo screamed.

Then the sky turned blood-red.

Shredder's spine-tingling laugh echoed through the shadows. Leo turned to face him. He could only see Shredder's eyes, brightly lit, like those of some possessed monster. Leo covered his face, afraid to look at the figure towering over him.

Shredder smacked him to the ground. Hard.

Anxious and injured, Leo summoned the strength to look up.

Shredder dragged his claws against the wall, leaving a trail of sparks as he stomped toward Leo. "There is no place you can run, no place you can hide," Shredder hissed. "You think you're ready to face me?" He snarled, raising his blades.

Leo covered his body as best he could. But it was no use. Shredder slashed him.

Splinter's eyes shot open. He sat up in bed, his heart still pounding from the nightmare. It took him a moment to realize it was all just a dream. . . .

Leo was fine. He hadn't been slashed.

The alleyway faceoff had never happened.

All of his sons were in the next room, hidden away from danger.

But were they safe?

No. As long as the Shredder was out there, they would never be safe.

Splinter collected himself and controlled his

fears, then opened the door. He made a surprising discovery.

The Turtles were gearing up to hit the surface.

"Where are you going?" Splinter demanded.

"Heading out for our evening patrol," Leo answered.

"There will be *no* patrol!" Splinter roared.

The Turtles were caught off guard. They weren't used to hearing Master Splinter like this. Something was very wrong.

"Last time you fought the Shredder you barely escaped with your lives!" Splinter reminded them.

"But, Sensei, next time we'll be ready!" Raph assured him.

Splinter wasn't satisfied. He knew his sons were far from ready to face a threat so great. To illustrate his point, he caught Raph in a surprise ninja-hold and held him there with ease.

"You will stay down here until you are ready," Splinter decreed. "No patrol. No games. *No rest!* There is only training. Starting now."

CHAPTER 16

For the next few weeks, the Turtles trained in the *dojo* day and night. At first, they missed little things like playing video games and skateboarding. But after countless exhausting practice sessions, all they wanted was some sleep.

"More, Sensei?" Mikey asked.

"Yes. More."

It seemed like there was no end in sight. Donnie and Mikey fought to keep their eyes open and summoned whatever strength they had left for the next run of *tenchi* throws—an ancient *ninjutsu* defense technique. They limply ran toward Leo and Raph, letting them toss them to the ground, barely putting up a fight.

"There is no intention in your strikes," barked

Splinter. "Do it again! We will practice all night if we have to!"

"We *have* been practicing all night," Donnie muttered, noticing Mikey was fast asleep on the floor beside him, snoring away. It would have been cute had it not summoned the wrath of Sensei!

"Wake him up," Splinter scolded.

The promise of causing Mikey bodily harm was enough to give Raph a much-needed energy boost. "Gladly," he obeyed.

Raph lifted Mikey in the air and body-slammed him down like a pro wrestler.

"Aah!" Mikey screamed as he snapped awake. "Shredder's here!"

"Relax," Leo told him. "You were just having a nightmare."

"Aren't we all?" Raph pointed out.

"Sensei, can we rest for a sec?" Donnie pleaded.

Splinter's eyes narrowed. He realized he was working his sons to the bone. But, he thought, if that was what it took to keep them alive, then there was no other way.

"Rest? The Shredder will not *rest* until you are all dead!" Splinter declared.

"Sensei, we've been training nonstop for weeks with hardly any sleep," Leo protested. "They need a break."

Not one to be shown up in front of Sensei, Raph cut in. "Like you don't?" he challenged.

"That's right, Raph; I don't," Leo replied.

"Then I'll give you a break," Raph said, cracking his knuckles. He shoved Leo. Suddenly, Splinter knocked down all his sons in a flurry of expert *ninjutsu* moves. The Turtles were all flat on their shells before they knew what hit them.

"If I were the Shredder, none of you would be breathing right now. Understand?" Splinter said angrily.

The Turtles caught their breath and sat up one by one. It was clear their sensei was right. If they were going to stand a chance against an expert ninja master, they were going to need more training.

Splinter watched Mikey fall into a deep sleep, snoring on Leo's shoulder.

"Perhaps a brief rest is in order," Splinter admitted. "We will resume later."

The moment Splinter left the *dojo,* the Turtles gave in to the need to sleep and shut their eyes. They'd never felt so exhausted in their entire lives.

"We're all gonna die!" a voice cried from the television set.

It was an episode of _Space Heroes,_ Leo's favorite show. He had it playing while he practiced some new _katana_ techniques. Leo watched as Captain Ryan, the leader of an intergalactic crew of deep-space explorers, got hit with an anxiety ray that sent him into a severe panic attack.

Leo knew exactly how Captain Ryan felt.

Leo didn't want to admit it to his brothers, but the truth was he was as frightened as the rest of them. Just thinking about Shredder gave him a chill. He knew it was best to keep his mind occupied with other things. Fun things.

Like _Space Heroes._

But just as Leo began to lose himself in Captain Ryan's outer-space adventures, a ninja star flew across the room and hit the Power button, shutting the TV off.

He turned to see Raph behind him, grinning.

"Hey! What are you doing?" Leo demanded.

"Oh, sorry. It was Spike's idea," Raph said as he fed his pet turtle, Spike, another leaf. "He said *Space Heroes* is too stupid for him."

"That's saying something, considering he hangs out with you all day," Leo blurted out.

That got Raph seething. His foul mood was nothing out of the ordinary, but the recent lack of sleep due to weeks of intense training had clearly turned him into an even bigger grump.

"Leo, you've angered Spike," Raph said calmly, but then his own anger erupted. "Now I'm gonna mop the floor with your face!"

"All right, Raph, cool off," Leo said.

Just then, Mikey popped up out of nowhere. "I can help with that!"

He pulled a water balloon from behind his shell and nailed Raph with it!

Mikey juggled two more water balloons, boasting, "Dr. Prankenstein strikes again!" He did a little happy dance until a drenched and unhappy Raph stepped up to him.

Mikey should've run far away. Instead, he said, "Dude, you should see your face right now! You look *so* mad!"

"Okay, Spike, you'll like *this* show," Raph said, making fists. "It's called *Does Mikey Bend That Way?*"

While Leo watched Raph chase Mikey around the room, it finally dawned on him: they were all dealing with this high-pressure situation in their own ways.

He retreated into his favorite TV show . . . while Mikey let off steam by having fun and pulling pranks . . . which let Raph relax the way he knew best: by beating Mikey senseless.

Hey, if that's what helps them cool off . . . , he thought. Which left him to wonder how Donnie was dealing with all this.

Leo, Raph, and Mikey found Donnie hidden behind a giant welding mask, tucked away in the corner of his lab. Holding a white-hot welding torch, he knelt in front of a strange-looking vehicle: a rust-covered jalopy with exposed seats pilfered from various junkyards, ill-fitting tires, and four separate steering wheels. His brothers thought it looked like a deformed wreck of a car. But to Donnie, it was a thing of beauty.

"You're still working on that go-kart?" Raph teased.

Donnie flipped his helmet up. "It's not a go-kart," he corrected him. "It's an all-terrain patrol buggy with detachable sidecars."

Mikey was confused. "Dude, hasn't Splinter been riding us hard enough? You've got to find a way to relax."

"We all deal with stress in different ways, Mikey," Leo pointed out.

"Yeah, this is how I deal," Donnie agreed.

"Well, this is how *I deal*," Mikey proclaimed, hurling another water balloon across the room. He was aiming for Leo . . .

. . . but hit Donnie instead!

Dripping wet, Donnie took off his welding helmet and starting chasing Mikey around the lab.

Pounding Mikey seems to be the most popular stress-reliever in the sewer, Leo mused.

As Mikey ran for his life, he calculated out loud. "Dr. Prankenstein's score: two bros hit, one more to go. You're next, Leo! And don't forget, Dr. Prankenstein makes house calls!"

CHAPTER 18

While the Turtles were hiding out, April was sneaking around with a large pepperoni pie in hand. Her plan was simple: impersonate a pizza delivery girl.

She stepped up to an old building. From the outside, it looked like a dilapidated fortune-cookie factory, but everyone on this side of town knew better—this was the secret hideout of the meanest gang in town, the Purple Dragons. April got into character and knocked on the door.

Sid, the most muscle-bound member of the gang, answered the door. Just behind him, at a table, were the other Purple Dragons—Fong and

Tsoi—glaring at her for interrupting their card game.

Lowering her voice, April asked, "Did somebody here order a totally delicious pizza?"

"No," Sid grunted. "Beat it."

"You sure? The guy who *paid* on the phone gave me this address," April lied, continuing to disguise her voice and force the pizza on Sid. She took a moment, and then for effect, added, "Maybe it's a block over? I'm so confused."

Sid suddenly changed his tune. "Oh, *that* pizza. Yeah, that's ours."

He gladly accepted the pizza and brought it inside—completely unaware that a tiny spy transmitter was hidden on the bottom of the box.

April left, activating her phone and opening up the Teen Spy app. She popped her headphones in and was able to listen in on the Purple Dragons' conversation within seconds. She pressed the Record button.

"Check it out, free pizza!" she heard Sid say.

Then she heard Fong yell at him, "Sit down and deal, Sid."

April smiled. She had successfully planted a

bug inside the Purple Dragons' hideout with nothing but a cheap disguise and a pepperoni pizza. Mission accomplished!

CHAPTER 19

Back at the Turtles' *dojo,* Leo was leading his brothers through a *ninjutsu* training exercise.

"Hoko no Kamae!" he commanded, which was Japanese for "bear stance." Leo held his arms up like a bear, feet shoulder-width apart. He waited for his brothers to follow along. They all did. Except Raph.

"Raph!" Leo shouted. *"Hoko no Kamae!"*

"Hoko no way!" Raph replied with his arms folded in protest. He was fed up. "It's bad enough Splinter's driving us into the ground. Now you, too?"

Leo broke stance to have a heart-to-heart with his bros. He couldn't blame Raph for feeling the way he did. They were under a lot of pressure.

But now was not the time to forget the threat that awaited them on the surface.

"We have to keep training," Leo told them. "Because right now, we don't stand a chance against Shredder."

"Yeah," Mikey said, a look of horror on his face. "And he's up there. Somewhere. Waiting for us!" The thought of that alone was enough to give Mikey the heebie-jeebies. He shuddered and added, "I just freaked myself out."

Then Donnie threw his two cents in. "I hate to say it, but the fact that we've been lying low might be the only reason we're still alive."

"Exactly," Leo agreed. "So until we're ready, we stay down here."

Suddenly, April was by his side.

"Unfortunately," she said, showing her phone to the guys, "that's not an option."

With the Turtles and Master Splinter huddled together, April played the spy recording she'd made of the Purple Dragons.

"We're meeting Shredder tonight. He's got a plan to destroy the Turtles." It's was Fong's voice.

Then they heard Sid ask, "How? He doesn't even know where they are."

"He says they're in the sewers somewhere and that's all he needs to know to wipe them out—"

April stopped the recording.

For a moment, no one spoke. The Turtles looked to their sensei for guidance, comfort, a kind word—*anything* to break the thick silence in the lair. As a wise ninja master, Splinter had trained himself to never show emotion. But everyone could see that the news had shaken him to his core.

"Our home is no longer safe," he said gravely. "Shredder must be stopped."

"How can we stop a plan we don't know?" Leo asked his sensei.

Like a star ninja pupil, Leo never took his eyes off Master Splinter, even though he sensed Mikey was readying a water balloon beside him. It might not have been the best time to continue the Dr. Prankenstein prank war, but Leo wasn't about to let Mikey get him. He quickly threw a ninja star and popped the balloon while it was still in Mikey's hand, drenching him good!

Raph ignored Mikey's shenanigans and tried to reason with Master Splinter. "We have to go topside and find out what they're planning."

"Raph's right," Leo said. "There's no other way."

Splinter nodded. He knew he couldn't keep his sons locked in the sewers anymore. If they were going to survive this war, they were going to have to find danger before it found them!

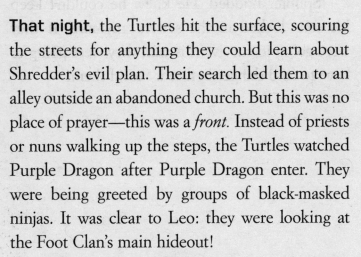

CHAPTER 20

That night, the Turtles hit the surface, scouring the streets for anything they could learn about Shredder's evil plan. Their search led them to an alley outside an abandoned church. But this was no place of prayer—this was a *front*. Instead of priests or nuns walking up the steps, the Turtles watched Purple Dragon after Purple Dragon enter. They were being greeted by groups of black-masked ninjas. It was clear to Leo: they were looking at the Foot Clan's main hideout!

"This is the place," Leo said, giving his brothers the signal to come closer and form a huddle.

Leo was shoved forward as his brothers rushed up behind him at once. They were way too close for comfort. Donnie and Raph were practically shell to shell!

"Donnie, you're crowding me," Raph grunted.

"Sorry," Donnie replied, backing off. But the moment he moved, he accidentally bumped into a trash can. Mikey screamed.

The other Turtles gave him the death stare for making so much noise. Was he trying to get them discovered?

"Sorry," Mikey said sheepishly. "All that Splinter-talk about how we're not ready has me thinking: *maybe* we're in over our heads."

"You're always in over your head," Raph said coldly.

"I'm saying now we *all* are," Mikey responded. "And that scares me."

Leo tried to comfort him. "It's okay to be scared, Mikey. Raph is scared, too."

"I'm not scared," Raph countered.

And then, just as Leo was about to prove how scared Raph actually was, a monstrous voice growled, "You should be."

Leo was the first to see the deformed figure at the end of the alley: it was a blur of fur, a hideous dog-man with bulging muscles and one gigantic fist. The mutant walked like a man and sounded very familiar. It was their old enemy, Chris Bradford!

"Look what I found . . . four soon-to-be ex-Turtles," the Bradford mutant snarled, seemingly growing bigger with every step it took, until he towered over them.

Mikey shrank behind his brothers. "I'm sure glad it's okay to be scared," he said, his voice quavering with fear.

"You and me both," Donnie agreed, trying to back away from the Bradford Mutant.

They needed a plan—an escape plan. Leo tried to keep his head, but he found it difficult to concentrate with an enormous mutant staring him down. Being in a dead-end alley made them sitting ducks. The only way to get out was to face this monstrosity head-on.

Leo drew his *katanas*. "This is no time to panic," he told his brothers.

The Bradford Mutant stepped closer. He seemed to be ten feet tall.

"He keeps getting taller!" Mikey exclaimed.

"Then I'll cut him down to size," Leo said, leaping up to unleash his airborne *katana* attack.

He swung the blades downward with all his strength and—*SLAM!*—the Bradford Mutant effortlessly blocked the blow with his impenetrable, two-ton fist.

This wasn't going to be easy. Leo had no choice but to backflip out of the fray, retreating to his brothers. "Uh, let's stick together on this one," he said, now just as frightened as they were.

THWACK-THWACK!

Donnie delivered a series of fierce *bo* staff strikes, trying to distract the dog-man on one side while Leo went to work on the other! But power punches and speed kicks appeared to do nothing to the monster. He overpowered Donnie and nearly crushed him with his massive fist. Then he swatted Leo around like a puny rag doll.

Seeing his brothers losing their ground, Mikey opted for the high road—and wrapped his *nunchucks* around a power line. Hanging on for dear life, he zip-lined down. He slid with both feet out, ready to deliver a forty-mile-per-hour dropkick, but the Bradford Mutant stopped him cold, using his gargantuan fist like a battering ram. He grabbed Mikey and tossed him to the back of the alley as easily as skipping a stone.

Picking his head up off the ground in time to see Mikey sail through the sky, Donnie yelled, "This is hopeless!"

"Hey, stay in the game!" Leo shouted back, trying to rally.

"I just wanna keep my head *on my body*!" Donnie screamed.

The Turtles were losing this fight badly. They were on the defensive, using their remaining strength to dodge the dog-man's crushing punches.

Raph was getting angry at his brothers. "C'mon!" he yelled. "What are we retreating for?"

The Bradford Mutant delivered a haymaker to Raph's jaw that sent him flying into a Dumpster.

"*That's* a good reason," Raph admitted in a punch-drunk daze.

Backing up toward the wall, Leo looked at each of his brothers, trying to think up their next plan of attack. How were they going to survive this? Their weapons were scattered. They had no strength left. All they had remaining in their arsenal were . . . Mikey's smoke bombs! Maybe they had an escape plan after all!

"Mikey! Smoke!" Leo commanded.

Realizing he was about to help them perform a daring, last-second escape, Mikey grabbed one of his homemade ninja smoke bombs. But he was so nervous, it slipped right out of his hands! A teensy poof of purple dust came out before the smoke bomb rolled into the sewer.

"What was that?" Raph asked.

"I'm stressed!" Mikey answered. "Excuse me if my aim's a little off!"

"How hard is it to hit the ground?!" Raph roared, throwing his own smoke bomb, which rolled weakly into the gutter.

Mikey felt vindicated! "Not so easy, is it?"

Leo couldn't hold off the Bradford Mutant anymore. His brothers were too busy fighting each other to help him fight off the dog-man.

"Oh, for the love of—" Leo said, and threw down his own smoke bomb.

It worked! The Bradford Mutant was left alone and confused in the alley, his prey disappearing into purple air.

CHAPTER 21

Defeated, the Turtles found themselves back at the lair, sitting in silence with April and Master Splinter. Their battle with the Bradford Mutant had left them hurting, and worst of all, ashamed. They were no closer to discovering Shredder's plan. Their home, along with everyone and everything in it, was in danger.

Leo sighed. "We couldn't do anything right."

"Dogpound was just too powerful," Mikey said sadly. "I came up with that name because he's a dog, and he pounded us into the—"

"We get it," Leo interrupted. "I don't see how we're going to get close to that Purple Dragon meeting now."

"Maybe we just need to find a new place to

hide. I hear the sewers in Florida are nice this time of year," Donnie suggested.

"No," April protested, which made them all look up. Judging by the seriousness in her voice and the determination on her face, she had a plan.

"I'm not letting you guys give up," she said, knowing the last thing they wanted to do was go back up to the surface. "*I'll* spy on the meeting."

Her suggestion was met with a wave of *nooooo*'s from the Turtles. There was no way they were going to let April risk her life.

"I can do this," she pleaded, looking at Master Splinter. "You've been training me to be a *kunoichi.*"

"But only for a few weeks!"

"What choice do we have? Shredder's going to attack your home, and we need to find out how. And I'm the only one who can do it," she declared.

No one wanted to admit it, but they all knew she was right. The bad guys would be expecting four Turtles, not a redheaded high school girl.

CHAPTER 22

A short while later, April found herself disguised as a pizza delivery girl again.

The Turtles watched from a nearby rooftop. The plan was simple: plant a pizza inside the Foot Clan's hideout with a hidden transmitter and listen in on Shredder's evil plans. It had worked for April before, but Donnie wasn't convinced.

"I don't like this," he said.

"Me neither," Mikey agreed. "Giving the enemy a free pizza?"

They watched April knock on the front door.

A Foot Soldier answered, and April launched into her spiel. "Did somebody here order a totally delicious—"

The Foot Soldier slammed the door in April's face before she could finish. She turned back down the alley and removed her T-Phone from her pocket. T-Phones were high-tech smartphones that Donnie had built for the Turtles and April. She called Leo. "Looks like the Foot Clan are smarter than the Purple Dragons," she reported.

Mikey sighed with relief. "At least we've still got the pizza!"

But April wasn't ready to call it quits. She eyed the old church building, looking for a way in.

"I'm not done yet," she said, hanging up the phone.

April spotted an open window that led into the hideout, but it was several stories up. She'd have to scale the fire escape next door just to *try* to leap over to it. It was a risky move, but it was her only choice.

Donnie watched April run to the opposite building. "What is she doing?"

Mikey peered over the roof in time to watch April throw her baseball cap and the pizza into a Dumpster.

"No, not the pizza!" Mikey lamented. "She's gone rogue!"

April ran up to the building and knocked on the door. An old man answered.

Lowering her voice, April launched into character. "Sir, I'm with the Firefighters Association." She flashed her school ID as if it were a badge. "We've received reports of some faulty wiring in this building. Mind if I have a look-see?"

Baffled, the old man said, "Well, I don't think—"

April shoved her way past him, heading inside and upstairs to the fire escape.

As he watched April climb out the second-floor window, Donnie had stars in his eyes. "She's so cool."

April stood on the guardrails of the fire escape, ready to put her *kunoichi* skills to the test. From this height, the jump over to the Foot Clan building looked like a one-way trip to the hospital, but she knew she had to make it.

April gulped, summoned her courage, and vaulted across the alley.

Her foot missed the ledge, but she managed to grab the edge and haul herself through the open window.

She was in the Foot Clan's hideout.

CHAPTER 23

April couldn't believe her eyes.

Down below, Shredder stood on a walkway over a floor-wide moat. Swimming inside it was the slimy, fish-faced Xever Mutant, a six-foot-long monstrosity that was now trapped in captivity like a pet.

April hugged the wall, trying to stay as quiet as possible while Shredder addressed his followers: the Foot Clan, the Purple Dragons, and his new mutant guard dog, Dogpound.

She carefully took out her T-Phone and dialed so Leo could listen in.

"Five of you will hijack a tanker truck coming down Houston Street in approximately fifteen minutes," Shredder announced. "It's filled with

an extremely rare chemical, so you will not get another chance."

Across the street, the Turtles listened closely.

"Chemical? What chemical?" Raph asked.

"How about we listen and find out?" Donnie argued.

"How about I break my shell on your knee?" Raph threatened.

Leo glowered at his brothers. "How about you two shut it for a minute while we try to hear the evil plan?!"

That got them to quiet down, but it was too late. They only caught the tail end of the plan.

". . . which will destroy them once and for all. Now go!" they heard the voice on the phone say.

"We missed it! Nice going, guys," Leo scolded them.

Donnie was more concerned about April at the moment.

"We've got to get her out," he said.

"No," Leo said firmly. "If we rush in there, we put her at risk. We wait."

On the street, Dogpound led the group of Foot Soldiers and Purple Dragons to a van waiting by the curb. They didn't notice April quietly slip out after them, then duck behind a Dumpster in the alley.

"I'm gonna hitch a ride," she whispered to the Turtles over the phone. "See where they go."

"No. You've done enough!" Leo replied. "Now get out of there!"

April slid into the shadows, unaware that Dogpound was scanning the darkness, his ears pricked up at the sound of their voices. His heightened senses were detected her breathing . . . *her scent.*

April sat, waiting for her chance to follow the van. Just when she thought the coast was clear, she looked up. The snarling mutant was looming over her, baring his razor-sharp fangs.

It was so quick, she didn't even have time to scream.

The Turtles saw it all from their perch.

"No!" Donnie yelled.

The Turtles hopped from the rooftop, their

sights set on the van. Every passing second meant life or death for April.

They hit the street and sprinted full speed. Down the block, they could see Dogpound strapping April into the van's passenger seat.

The Turtles ran harder.

Donnie watched in horror as Dogpound's van disappeared into the night.

"We're too late!" he cried.

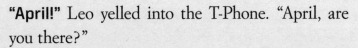

CHAPTER 24

"April!" Leo yelled into the T-Phone. "April, are you there?"

There was nothing on the other end but static.

Donnie tried to reason with him. "She's not going to answer. What do we do?"

Leo started to panic. He couldn't breathe. He didn't have a plan. He began to think out loud.

"We've got to get April out of that van. But Dogpound's in the van. And we're not ready to fight that guy!" Leo's eyes darted from brother to brother. "Splinter was right! We should've stayed below!"

Raph had never seen Leo act like this. Normally, he would've made fun of him or knocked him back to reality. But this was different. Leo was clearly losing control. He knew there was only one way to get through to him: *Space Heroes*.

"I can't believe I'm saying this," Raph muttered to himself. He turned to Leo, lowered his voice, and snapped, "Get it together, Captain! You're our leader, so act like one!"

That made Leo feel like a hero.

"You're right, Raph." Leo smiled. Then, with a newfound confidence, he quoted the rest of the scene back to Raph, "That was the anxiety ray talking."

The rest of the Turtles were relieved to see him back in fighting shape—even if it meant sitting through a dorky *Space Heroes* reenactment.

"Let's save April," Leo said.

"And our home," Raph agreed.

"But we'll never catch them on foot," Donnie pointed out.

Leo didn't seem worried at all now. His eyes were focused on the road ahead. "Oh, we're not going on foot."

At sixty-five miles per hour, Donnie's patrol buggy zipped out of the lair and onto the downtown streets.

"It's not ready!" Donnie shouted over the dull hum of the road.

And he was right. The entire vehicle rattled the moment Leo hit the gas. The tires were wobbly, there was no windshield, and the seats were uncomfortable. But it was their best chance of catching up to Dogpound, intercepting the tanker, and rescuing April.

"This thing is awesome!" Mikey shouted with the wind whipping his face. "Does it have a radio?"

"No, it does not have a radio!" Donnie yelled impatiently. He tinkered with a stray wire that

was poking out below the dashboard and hastily reminded them, "I'm telling you, it's not ready!"

"Seems ready to me!" Leo said confidently—just before pulling the steering wheel off!

The other Turtles all looked on nervously, their hearts racing.

"Okay, let's get busy." Leo said, frantically trying to shove the steering wheel back into place.

Dogpound's van sped down to Houston Street.

April, still strapped in, struggled to break free, but it was no use. The Foot Soldiers were holding her down, and she could barely move a muscle. All she could do was watch helplessly as they drove through red light after red light.

They were gaining on the tanker trunk. Once they were in position, Dogpound leaped off the van and landed in front of the tanker, blocking its path.

The tanker's driver hit the brakes.

"Get out!" Dogpound growled, ripping the

tanker's door off with one brutal swipe. The driver ran screaming into the street.

A Foot Soldier dashed over from the van, taking the wheel of the tanker. Dogpound planted himself on the side of the truck as it drove off, pleased that the hijacking had been successful.

"Call Shredder," he told the Foot Solider in the driver's seat. "Tell him we've acquired the tanker and we're on our way. No problems encountered."

The blasting sound of a revving engine made Dogpound look up at the street ahead—just as an off-road vehicle spun around the corner into their lane! The Turtles' patrol buggy raced directly at the tanker.

"Hold that call," Dogpound boomed. "Run them down!"

"Raph, get ready!" Leo said, speeding up.

"Ready for what?" Raph asked.

"THIS!" Leo shouted.

Right as the two vehicles were about to collide head-on, Leo pulled a release lever that split the buggy into two separate cars!

"Whoa!" Raph screamed, turning his own steering wheel to safety and swerving past the oncoming truck.

Leo and Raph's buggies zoomed down either side of the tanker in one wild high-speed move. They spun around, tires tearing asphalt. Now they were behind the truck.

Raph pulled up alongside Leo's buggy, pacing him. "You could've given me a *little* warning!"

"Where's the fun in that?" Leo winked.

As they closed in on the tanker, Donnie read the warning on the back of the vehicle.

"*Chlorosulfonic acid?*" he read aloud. "Oh no! Leo, I think I figured out Shredder's plan! That acid reacts violently with water!"

Leo gasped. "If he dumps it in the sewer—"

"It'll all be incinerated in seconds," Donnie finished, cutting him off. "Including the lair!"

"And Splinter!" Leo realized. "We gotta stop them!"

Eyeing the other lever on his console, Leo knew what he had to do next. He turned to Donnie in the backseat. "You and Raph stay with the van and save April!"

He looked at Raph's buggy, catching Mikey's eye. "Mikey, you're coming with me! We have to stop that tanker!"

"Uh, if you haven't noticed, I'm stuck with Raph!" Mikey pointed out from the backseat.

"No problem," Raph said, taking a cue from Leo. Without warning, he yanked the detach lever on his buggy and shot Mikey out on his own set of wheels!

"Whoaaaaa!!!" Mikey yelled, barely getting his vehicle under control.

"That *was* fun," Raph admitted.

"Told ya," Leo responded, detaching Donnie's sidecar as well.

All four vehicles zoomed toward their targets, racing to save the day!

Gunning their engines, Leo and Mikey caught up with Dogpound and the tanker. They needed a way to stop this bomb on wheels from getting any closer to the sewers they called home.

Leo noticed a firing switch on his patrol buggy and sent a silent thank-you to Donnie. "Mikey, let's slow this thing down! Fire grappling hooks!"

"Got it!" Mikey said, his finger already on the button.

They fired at the same time, smiling as the hooks plunged into the truck with a direct hit. They waited for the tanker to be pulled back, but nothing happened.

The grappling-hook chains weren't connected to anything! They unraveled uselessly, falling to the street with a thud.

"Donnie did say the buggies weren't ready!" Mikey reminded him.

"I know!" Leo grunted.

Maybe taking this tanker down wasn't going to be so easy.

Speeding alongside the Foot Clan's van, Donnie spotted April in the passenger seat. There was no telling where the soldiers planning on taking her, so he had to get her out of there—fast!

Donnie pulled a ninja smoke bomb out of his shell and got his buggy close enough for April to hear him over the headwind.

"Hold your breath, April!" Donnie instructed.

POOF!

The smoke bomb exploded inside the van! The driver slowed down to keep control. Seeing an opportunity, Raph shot forward in his buggy, dropping a trail of jagged spikes along the road ahead. The van didn't have time to stop. It drove over the spikes, popping its tires instantly.

The second the van came screeching to a stop, Donnie and Raph sprang out of their buggies to rescue April.

"Let's club these Feet!" Raph shouted.

"I think they're called *Foots*," Donnie corrected him.

Raph readied his *sais*. "Just hit 'em."

The Foot Soldiers jumped out of the van, brandishing weapons. But it didn't matter. Donnie and Raph were just too fast for them. With a few quick punches, the Turtles made short work of their ninja enemies.

April kicked the passenger-side door open, knocking out one of the Purple Dragons in the process.

"Nice shot!" Donnie said, untying her.

"Nice wheels," April replied, geeking out over the patrol buggies.

"I built them, you know," Donnie bragged.

Donnie was feeling pretty proud of himself . . . until his buggy suddenly fell apart behind him.

"They're, uh, not ready yet." He blushed.

CHAPTER 26

Dogpound jumped from the tanker truck and tore off a manhole cover to finish the job. As a human, he had failed Shredder time and time again. But now, as a mutant, Dogpound would finally make his master proud.

Leo and Mikey's buggies rolled into view and sped toward the tanker.

With a super-powered throw, Dogpound spun the manhole cover like a flying disc. Leo took his hands off the wheel and somersaulted into the air, saving himself at the last possible moment. The manhole cover sent Leo's cart spinning backward.

Mikey drove up in time to see Leo land safely on the street, right in front of Dogpound.

"Is that all you got?" Leo challenged, drawing his *katanas*.

Dogpound hunched over, ready to attack.

"I'd say that's a no," Mikey observed. He abandoned his buggy and leaped to Leo's side.

Dogpound balled his enormous fist and began swinging and punching away, trying to squash the Turtles. With every punch that missed, Dogpound smashed holes into the pavement, twisted streetlights into pretzels, and sent the Turtles flying into buildings.

Running out of places to hide, Leo and Mikey *poof*ed their way onto some nearby scaffolding to try to escape Dogpound's fury for a moment. Leo scanned the street below and saw a Foot Soldier setting up one of the tanker's hoses to pump acid into the sewers!

"Mikey, don't let him dump that acid!" Leo ordered.

As Mikey climbed back down to the street, Dogpound's fist grabbed the scaffold. The mutant started to pull his muscle-bound form up to Leo, but his immense weight nearly toppled the structure.

On the street, Mikey fought the Foot Soldier as best he could, trying to keep him away from the acid-filled hose. Leo hopped down to help. But Dogpound wasn't finished with him yet.

The beast chased after Leo. It picked up a parked car and swung it around easily. It nearly took Leo's head clean off his shell! Before Leo could strike back with his *katana,* Dogpound grabbed him by the wrist and threw him into the truck. Leo's sword accidentally sliced the tanker! The explosive acid—a putrid, neon-green goop—sprayed out like a geyser.

Something occurred to Leo as he watched the toxic fluid spray out. *What did Donnie say about this stuff? Explosive when mixed with water?*

"Mikey, throw the water balloon!" Leo yelled.

"What water balloon?" Mikey asked in an innocent voice.

"The one you were going to hit me with!" Leo answered.

Mikey's eyes widened. "Dude, you are *good!*" he exclaimed. He pulled a fat balloon from his shell and sent it soaring.

The water balloon popped and—

KABOOM!

The tanker erupted in a huge green explosion

that burned up all the acid instantaneously. The blast sent a shock wave that knocked everyone off their feet.

The sewers were saved!

When the smoke cleared, Leo stood up, searching for Dogpound. But there was no sign of him. He turned and looked at Mikey. He was proud of his brother. And right as he exclaimed "Nice shot, Mikey!" Mikey saw his chance and nailed Leo in the face with another water balloon.

"Dr. Prankenstein for the win!" he crowed.

"You had two of those?" Leo asked him, dripping with water. "Where do you keep them?"

Mikey waited for retaliation, but there was none. Leo was too happy about their victory to be annoyed.

"Looks like we missed the fireworks," said a voice.

They turned to see Raph and Donnie jogging up to join them.

"Donnie, the go-kart worked great. Nice job," Leo said.

"Thanks, Leo," Donnie replied. And then he

quickly reminded him, "Oh, and . . . it's a *patrol buggy*."

Whether or not they realized it, the four of them stood a little taller now. As they watched the tanker flames burn up the rest of the chemical, they felt like their fears and worries had also gone up in smoke. They had rescued their best friend, protected their home and their master, and defeated Dogpound.

They felt like they had reclaimed their power.

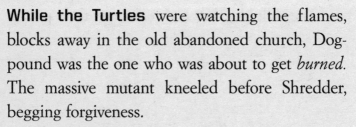

CHAPTER 27

While the Turtles were watching the flames, blocks away in the old abandoned church, Dogpound was the one who was about to get *burned.* The massive mutant kneeled before Shredder, begging forgiveness.

But Shredder wasn't exactly in a forgiving mood.

"They defeated you with *go-karts* and a water balloon," he growled with contempt.

Dogpound attempted to plead his case. "I know it sounds absurd, but—"

The sound of Shredder's gauntlet blades coming out was enough to stun Dogpound into silence. The ferocious mutant looked up, frightened to see Shredder aiming his knives straight at him.

"It won't happen again, Master," Dogpound yelped. "I promise you."

Dogpound could sense the rage swelling up behind Shredder's mask. Few had failed him so spectacularly and lived to see another day. Would this be the end of the line? Had Shredder finally run out of second chances to give to him?

Shredder came closer. "If you break that promise—"

SNIKT! Shredder slashed, slicing off the tip of one of Dogpound's backbone spikes.

The massive mutant squealed in pain. With that kind of a warning, Dogpound trembled like a scared puppy.

"I understand, Master," Dogpound said.

Shredder returned to his throne, showing Dogpound mercy by letting him live. For now.

The mutant mutt left the lair with his tail between his legs.

CHAPTER 28

It was Pizza Time back at the Turtles' lair. Mikey admired his slice, his mouth watering.

"Nothing says victory like the sweet taste of pizza," he announced proudly.

Right as Donnie was about to bite down on his slice, he caught a whiff of something odd. Something *stinky*.

"This pizza smells kind of funky. Where'd you get it?" he asked.

"It's the one April threw out," Mikey replied, oblivious.

All at once, the other Turtles spat their pizza out and tossed the slices aside, disgusted.

"What? We live in a sewer!" Mikey reminded his bros. "And now you're *clean freaks*?!" He gathered up their discarded slices, shrugging. "More for me."

Master Splinter entered the lair to join his sons. He was proud of them for their victory, but his stern face suggested he had something else on his mind.

"My sons, I owe you my gratitude . . . and an apology," he told them.

"An apology?" Leo asked.

"Fear clouded your minds. However, it was not Shredder who fueled that fear; it was *me*," Splinter confessed. "You overcame that fear and performed admirably."

Splinter looked at his sons with great pride. He could see they were deeply touched by his words. And he knew they'd be even more excited by the shocking announcement he was about to make.

"No training today," Splinter proclaimed.

The Turtles cheered, but Master Splinter stopped them with a warning.

"Unless Michelangelo throws that water balloon."

As Master Splinter turned and walked away, the Turtles all jumped on Mikey, tackling him to the ground to save the most important thing in their universe at that moment: *a much-needed day off.*

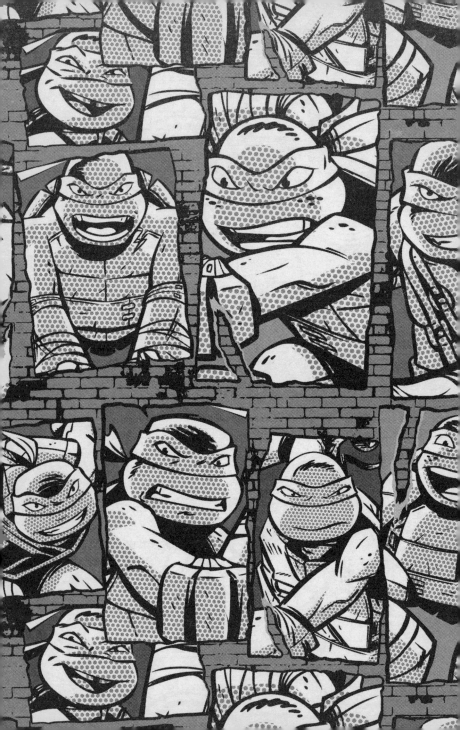